GW01457892

Poetry of Healing and Abuse

3rd EDITION

Sam Vaknin

The Author is NOT a Mental Health Professional.
The Author is certified in Counselling Techniques.

Editing and Design:

Lidija Rangelovska

A Narcissus Publications Imprint

Prague & Haifa 2022

Visit the Author's Web site	http://www.narcissistic-abuse.com
Facebook	http://www.facebook.com/samvaknin
	http://www.facebook.com/narcissismwithvaknin
YouTube channel	http://www.youtube.com/samvaknin
Instagram	https://www.instagram.com/vakninsamnarcissist/ (archive)
	https://www.instagram.com/narcissismwithvaknin/

Buy other books and video lectures about pathological narcissism and relationships with abusive narcissists and psychopaths here:

http://www.narcissistic-abuse.com/thebook.html

Buy Kindle books here:

http://www.amazon.com/s/ref=ntt_athr_dp_sr_1?_encoding=UTF8&field-author=Sam%20Vaknin&search-alias=digital-text&sort=relevancerank

CONTENTS

Throughout this book click on blue-lettered text to navigate to different chapters or to access online resources

Author Bio

Cutting to Existence

My little brother cuts himself into existence.

With razor tongue I try to shave his pain,

he wouldn't listen.

His ears are woollen screams, the wrath

of heartbeats breaking to the surface.

His own Red Art.

When he cups his bleeding hands

the sea of our childhood

wells in my eyes

wells in his veins

like common salt.

Return

Fearful Love

Cherubim turn swords,

cast flaming fig leaves

on a cursed ground.

With bruised heels

we labour

among the bitten,

festering fruits of our ignorance,

making thorns and thistles

of our crowns.

In the sweat of our faces,

a pheromonic resonance.

In our dusty hearts,

skinclad, in cleavage,

we hope to live forever,

flesh closed upon itself,

conceiving sorrow.

Our trees are pleasant to the sight

of gold and onyxstone

and every beast and fowl has its name

except for our nakedness.

In a garden of talking serpents,

cool days and lying Gods,

I betray you to the voice

and hide.   <u>Return</u>

In the concentration camp called Home

In the concentration camp called Home,

we report in striped pyjamas

to the barefeet commandant,

Our Mother orchestrating

our daily holocaust.

Burrowing her finger-

-nails through my palms,

a scream frozen between us,

a stalactite of terror

in the green caves of her eyes

there, sentenced to forced labour:

to mine her veins of hatred

to shovel her contempt

to pile scorn upon scorn

beating(s) a path.

At noon, Our Mother

leads us to the chambers

naked, ripples of flesh

she turns on the gas

and watches our hunger

as her food devours us.

Return

Prague at dusk

The City laces its inhabitants in shades of grey. Oppressively close to the surface, some of us duck, others simply walk carefully, our shoulders stooped, trying to avoid the monochrome rainbow, somewhere over, at the end of the hesitant drizzle.

The City rains itself on us, impaled on one hundreds towers, on a thousand immolated golden domes. We pretend to not see as it bleeds into the river. We just cross each other in ornate street corners, ambushed from behind dilapidated structures.

We don't nod our heads politely anymore. We are not sure whether they will stay connected to their lolling bodies if we do.

It is at such times that I remember an especially sad song, interlaced with wailing.

Wall after wall, turret after turret, I re-visit her. It is there, in that city, which is not Muslim, nor Jewish, or Christian, not entirely modern, nor decidedly antique that I met her.

And the pain.

Passing Ships

We are ships that pass in pitch darkness, blowing horns of despair and need, trying to avoid the inevitable collision of intimacy, the lifeboats of cheating and emotional absenteeism at the ready.

There is no moon on our ocean, just the churning waves of loneliness, the froth of our relationship sprayed thin across our lives, as insubstantial as the dreamworld we call our mind.

Lone seagulls of pity oversee us, necklaced albatrosses of empathy and love, phosphorous fish gaze up, their mouths agape at our oddness.

At times, we shipwreck, outcast on our islands, and we wonder at the exoticism of our selves, the hopelessness of memory: such strange beasts we are, such miracles, once in our lifetimes, a roll of DNA, or an experiment gone awry.

We set sail into penumbral seas in a doomed quest for sun and flowers. And yet it is our forlornness that renders us so painfully beautiful to behold even in the absence of any light.

<u>Return</u>

The Old Gods Wander

your promised lands

with reticence.

Grey, forced benevolence.

They shrug their crumpled robes,

extend in venous hand

black cornucopia.

You're fighting back, it's evident,

bony protrusions, a thumping chest,

the clamming up of sweaty pearls.

They aim at your Olympian head.

There, in the meadows of your mind,

grazing on dewy hurt,

they defecate a premonition

of impending doom.

Return

Moi Aussi

I need to know you

even as I never know my self

that phantom ache

of amputated innocence

You,

the stirrings of a curtain, dust

settling on sepia cuckoo clocks

covers obscuring

Perhaps one day you will become

a benign sentence

an agency

through which to be.

Return

When You Wake the Morning

When you wake the morning

red headed children shimmer in your eyes.

The venous map

of sun drenched eyelids

flutters

throbbing topography.

Your muscles ripple.

Scared animals burrow

under your dewy skin.

Frozen light sculptures

where wrinkles dwell.

Embroidered shades,

in thick-maned tapestry.

Your lips depart in scarlet,

flesh to withering flesh,

and breath in curved tranquillity

escapes the flaring nostrils.

Your warmth invades my sweat,

your lips leave skin regards

on my humidity.

Eyelashes clash.

Return

Tableaux (on van Gogh)

Listening to a scarlet sink, detached

an ear, still glistening wax,

in bloody conch.

The gaping flesh.

Wild scattered eyes

fiorcing the mirror,

Light ricochets from trembling blade

(it's gaslight evening and the breeze ...)

Behind his stooping shoulders,

a painted room ablaze

the dripping composition of his blood.

The winding crowd

inflates the curtains inwards,

sails of a flying Dutchman.

Return

Sally Ann

I wrote, Sally Ann, I wrote:

Shot from the cannon of abuse
as unwise missiles do.

Course set.

Explosive clouds that mark
your video destination.

Experts interpret,
pricking with laser markers,
inflated dialects
of doom.

Hitting the target, you
splinter, a spectacle
of fire and of smoke.

The molten ashes,
the cold metallic remnants,
the core...

A peace accord
between you and your self.

Return

Prowling

The little things we do together

to give up life.

The percolating coffee,

your aromatic breath,

the dream that glues

your eyelids to my cheek.

We both relent relentlessly.

Your hair flows to its end,

a natural cascade,

a velvet avalanche

buries my hands.

In motion paralyzed,

we prowl each other's

hunting grounds.

Day breaks, our backs

turned to the light

in dark refusal.

Return

Switching

Vaknin packets switching
'twixt all my addresses.
Servers process my roots,
my names
caught in their web.
Routed to their domain,
I am browsed by
people downloading
stale pains
uploaded fresh
and dripping bytes.

Return

Getting Old

The sageing flesh,
a wrinkled vicedom.
The veined reverberation
of a life consumed.
On corneas imprinted
with a thousand dreams,
now stage penumbral plays
directed by a sight receding
and a brain enraged.
To fall, as curtains call,
to bow the last,
rendered a sepia image
in a camera obscured,
a line of credits,
fully exhausted,
fully endured.

Return

Narcissism

The Toxic
waste of bottled anger
venomized.
Life belly up.
The reeds.
The wind is hissing
death
downstream,
a river holds
its vapour breath
and leaves black lips
of tar and fish
a bloated shore.

Strolling in the boneyard of my life:
bleached dreams,
mementoed ossuary of my insights.
On flaking fenceposts, impaled the child that I had been.
Peering from desiccated sockets, the Plague that's me:
dust-irrigated, arid tombstones,
a being eclipsed.

Stage 1, receding, jettisoned, stage 2, exiled velocity, stage 3, stage 3 ...
The armoured carapace.
Atremored.
In glinted envelope, pulsating, rarefied,
A fiery launch that crumbles into
velvet silence.
No comm.
On impact, just a
star rush,
the pullulating milky veins,
expired, crater-ridden scars.
What's in your call sign? Freedom? Friendship? Faith?
None, I think. I am over, out,
an iron shell,
tons in a matchbox,
frenetic revolutions,
ray bursts,
the stellar remnant

of collapse.

Return

Snowflake Haiku

Where I begin
your end
snowflake haikus
melt into
crystalline awareness.

I guard
your quivered sleep.
Your skin beats moisture.
The beckoning jugular
that is your mind.

My pointing teeth.

A universe
of frozen sharp relief,
the icy darts your voice
in my inebriated veins
in yours.

Return

A Hundred Children

Tell me about your sunshine
and the sounds of coffee
and of barefeet pounding the earthen floor
the creaking trees
and the skinned memory of hugs
you gave
and you received.

Sit down, yes, here,
the intermittent sobbing
of the shades
slit by your golden face.

Now listen to the hundred children
that are your womb.

I am among them.

Return

In Moist Propinquity

Hemmed in our bed,
in moist propinquity,
'tis night and starry
and the neighbourhood inebriated,
in the vomitary of our street.
A woman,
my stone-faced lover,
a woman and her smells.
The yellow haze of melancholy lampposts.
Your hair consumes you.

Return

Selfdream

At times, I dream myself besieged.
I rebel with the cunning of the weak.
I walk the shortcuts.
Tormentors clad
in blood-soaked black,
salute as I manipulate them
into realizing their abyss.
Some weep their sockets hollow,
or waive their thorns.
Much pain negotiated.
A trading of the wounds.
My chains carve metal
and I am branded.

Return

The Miracle of the Kisses

That night, the cock denied him thrice.
His mother and the whore downloaded him,
nails etched into his palms,
his thorny forehead glistening,
his body speared.
He wanted to revive unto their moisture.
But the nauseating scents of vinegar
and Roman legionnaires,
the dampness of the cave,
and then that final stone...
His brain wide open,
supper digested
that was to have been his last.
He missed so his disciples,
the miracle of their kisses.
He was determined not to decompose.

Return

Our Love Alivid

Our bloated love alivid

at the insolence of time

protests by falling in,

involuntarily committed.

You are the sadness

in my sepia nights.

I am in yours.

We correspond across

our dead togetherness.

Return

Synthetic Joy

Synthetic joy of wedding halls,

caked bride and groom,

a spewing orchestra,

metallic rings.

Exchanging aqueous looks,

thickset in exudate,

the relatives.

Mother exuding age,

a father pillaged by defeat,

a clutch of wombless matrons.

The light is ashen,

the food partitioned.

Soon, scene of soiled tables.

Soon, the relieved goodbyes.

Soon, the breathless breeding and the crumpled sheets.

The neon lights extinguished by the dawn.

Return

Twinkle Star

Twinkle star

of barren scape

and ashen craters.

Seething Ammonia winds.

The fine dust

of life forgone

on surface tensioned.

Beneath its crust

trapped oceans surge

in icy recollection.

It hurls its core

again the dimming sun's

depleted inattention.

Return

My Putrid Lover

My lover dreams

of acrid smells

and putrid tangs

I lick

(dishevelled hair adorns)

her feet

I scale

the shrink-warped body.

I vomit semen

that her lips ingest.

And youth defies her.

Return

Hebrew Love

Ahavat ha'akher ena ela	Loving another is merely
ahavat ha'ani ba'akher.	Loving Myself in another.
Ba'akher ani:	In the Other I:
Khesronot	Shortcomings
Ke'evim	Pains
Nikudei turpa	Vulnerabilities
Kabala lelo hatnaya of	the Unconditional Intercourse
Ahavim.	Love.
Lehitama bahem	Subsumed
Ulehatmia.	Engulfing.
Ulam shel mar'ot,	A Hall of Mirrors,
Gvulut ben shtei aratsot nokhriot,	Two Bounded States,
Ir prazot	an Open City
vehaohev basha'ar,	my Lover at its gates,
Gesher khovek	a Bridge hugging
tehomot,	an abyss,
Migdal mamri, kulo safa belula, wholly confounded language,	a tower, heaven reached,
Mabul.	a Deluge.
Verak anakhnu,	And only Us,
Shnayim beteiva venoakh	two of a sort,
li velakh.	an Ark, a Covenant. Return

Her Birthday

By my Love for You,

I am.

Overwhelmed.

I.   **Apology** ...

My Wife:

Sometimes I watch you from behind:

your shoulders, avian, aflutter.

Your ruby hands;

the feet that carry you to me

and then away.

I know I wrong You.

Your eyes black pools; your skin eruptions of what is

and could have been.

I vow to make you happy, but

my Hunchbacked Self

just tolls the bells

and guards you from afar.

II.   **... And Thanks**

In the wasteland that is Me

You flower.

Your eyes black petals strewn

across the tumbling masonry.

Your stem resists my winds.

Your roots, deep in my soil,

toil in murk to feed both you and me,

to nurture Us.

And every day a spring,

and every morn a sunshine:

you're in my garden,

you blossom day and night.

Your sculpted daint feels

in my hands like oneness.

III.　　In Toronto

So much is left unsaid between us.

Your crests of silence

fallen on my shores of pain.

IV.　　Dedication (9th Edition of "Malignant Self-love")

My Wife:

You are in every carefully measured space,

In every broken word

That we had mended with

The healing hyphens of our together-

-ness.

This book, the memory of us,

A record of survival

Against all odds.

Malignant Self- gives way to love, two points, we are:

Revisited.

V.   Happy 2014
(Dedication on the book "Macedonian Woodcarving")

Carved in the wood of our togetherness, entwined,

the chiseled hurt of us:

sprawled in your arms, my wounds

and your iconic smile,

Madonna of leaves and angels.

Only one unicorn we are,

sheltered behind the royal doors

to our love. And you?

My own Iconostasis.

VI.   Dedication (10th Edition of "Malignant Self-love")

In the tenth edition of our lives, we:

muscles aching,

voices raised,

backs bent upon

the pain of editing the past.

You in my studio, I in your night,

pecking at keyboards,

nearsighted, glazed.

And outside? Rain chases Sun

and cats among narcissi

and new life sprouts and old.

We leave behind only these sheaves

of paper children,

off spring.

VII.   **Remember Me**

Very often, I cannot remember me.

But I remember that you make me happy.

   You make me happy when:

      We watch a film together

      We eat your delicious food

      We talk (and talk and talk)

      You smile with enormous cheeks

      I hold your delicate bird-like hand in mine

      You run and stumble on the way to our bed

      You talk to and agree with or argue with yourself

      You make our apartment a home with gentle touch and souvenirs

      You return at night, flustered, excited, loving

      You listen to the birds, feed all the cats, talk to the dogs (they listen)

You make me very happy Lidija.

And this is why I am not back - because I never left.

In search for Sam, I am moving towards him - not away from you.

And in the dim, dreamlike existence that I lead,

in the turbulent whirlpool that I am,

a vortex and an apparition,

a sepia shadow of myself,

pure dust - from this nothingness,

for lack of another, better word, I feel.

I call it love. My love for you.

Having forgotten all else - even us - I remember only you,

and survive from one visit of yours to another,

knocking on echoed doors behind which I am not,

entombed,

scribbling furiously in a journal,

a diary that will never be written.

    Your Sam

VIII. The Traveller

Forty days and forty nights the journey lasted. Over mountains, across seas and lakes, traversing plane and prairie. Until the wearied traveller, famished, fatigued, and parched fell to the ground in a foreign land and stirred no more.

He didn't know how long his stupor lasted but, when he woke up at last, he beheld the most marvellous flower he had ever seen: at once fragile and strong, scented and beautiful, its petals colourful and shimmering in the sun.

The flower nodded gently in the breeze, brushing against the traveller's bristled cheeks. Invigorated, the journeyman got up, found a stream of water, drunk from it, and washed himself. He picked low-lying fruits for his meal and all the time he eyed the tiny flower with wonderment and gratitude: it gave him life and hope and beauty.

Weeks passed and the traveller decided to return to his home. He made preparations: packed his meagre possessions, scooped water into a basket made of bark, and assembled fruits of all kinds into a blanket he has tied to a stick he had improvised from a fallen branch.

Time came to depart, but the traveller could not leave without his flower. He gently and lovingly dug it out, wrapped it carefully in an earth-filled kerchief and embarked on his way.

When he reached his destination, his family and friends marvelled at the flower. He bought a plot of land, cultivated it meticulously, to make a new home for his flower, the saviour of his life.

But, as the days turned into weeks and the weeks to months, the flower withered. Its petals dimmed and fell, its proud stem stooped, its scent diminished and then vanished altogether. Perplexed and saddened, the traveller called upon the greatest botanist of the land and asked him to inspect the flower and render his opinion.

"No need" - responded the botanist - "for I have seen these things before. Some plants can flourish and thrive only in their native soil, where the right admixture of sunlight and water is available, where insects indigenous to these parts help them reproduce. Only there these flowers giveaway their natural gifts: their beauty and their scent. If you really love this flower, take it back to where you found it. Give it its life back as it has given you yours!"

And the traveller who loved the flower greatly did just that.

Never doubt my love for you, my beautiful flower and my life.

Sam, your traveller

10/8/2007---> forever

IX. 1138 – A Love Poem

On our rented porch,

above the starlit city,

the Sun sets in refracted wine.

We sip the silence,

quivering limbs entwined.

Pain harks to pain.

Bloodied

Beaten

Weary

Torn

We explore each other's

shrines, like pilgrims

in the holy land

of our Love.

X. Crimson Marriage

In your work-weary hands

you drew the squarish box

sheathed in crimson velvet

and you asked:

"Do you know what this is?"

"No," brows raised.

"It is your wedding ring,

but it doesn't fit you"

(When I finally tried it on after

15 years of naked finger).

And there was such resignation in your voice

as you contemplated with ashen eyes

this patinated relic of our

fading union.

The marriage I buried in the squarish box

sheathed in crimson velvet.

<u>Return</u>

To an Absent Wife

I went to my heart and enquired to know how to make you mine again,
But my heart was broken and I asked in vain.

I then spoke to my brain to learn how to rekindle our flame,
But my brain was busy dousing out my pain.

And I talked to friends and my mother too.
And I surfed the Net and read books a few.
For I saw your face in every cranny and nook.
And recalled your smile and the way you look.

So I typed my love on my mobile's face
And I send you this with my warm embrace.

Note: A "mobile" in the UK is a "cellphone" in the USA.

[Return](#)

Love, Face, Skin

Love

My deer, I am your headlights, the pool to your reflection.

I am the forest of your trees, the wind which sussurates your branches, the sepia foliage at your naked feet.

Face

I hold that precious orb in tremulous hands: the golden fleece, grey pools, a flaring nostril, your cornered lips aflutter.

My tongue makes love to your penumbral smoothness.

Skin

Sheathed in translucence you are, draped in the parchment of your life, a venous palimpsest, the sanguine estuaries, throbbing pulse.

I lay my hands on this partition, I knock, you let me in.

Solitary

A solitary letter ending
the alphabet.

Uncertain memories:
Did any of this happen?
Did I?
Was she?

A figure in a dream,
face blanked,
exchanged.

Where I should be,
her smells.
Her tastes.
Her sad, lopsided smile.

And now my being

reduced
to words:
mangled in writing,
spoken to bits,
disrupted by dial tones.

Between us time itself.

Return

Bladed Stalactite

Time has arrived.

Time is here.

Oh, Sam.

But the snow is great.

And you, bladed stalactite,

shredded your loved ones

Into a ticker-tape parade,

confettied aftermath of distant glories.

Sic transit.

Now that you are melting,

there is no one left

to gather your holy water

and to exorcise the demons

in the empty cave

that you had become.

Oh Sam. Oh Sam.

It is time already.

Return

A Memory of Salt

From behind him, always

Trailing, fatigued, uphill:

Two daughters,

The salvaged trinkets

Of a life inflamed

In brimstone.

A good man, her husband,

Hospitable,

Righteous,

On intimate terms with God.

But the minute she tried to

Capture their togetherness,

Turning her back on him for just an instance,

He made her into a memory of salt,

Gone with the first rain,

Melting seamlessly into the smoke

Of the furnace she used to call her home.

Her daughters, circling, uncorked the wine.

Return

Traces of a Haunted Woman

The sweaty bodies of men paint

hieroglyphs of her insanity.

Them that had penetrated her perforce

But never pierced her veil.

I watch her swirl like a dervish in heat.

I observe her floating gracelessly in alcohol placentas, all sepia, settled like a dust mote

in my eye.

If a woman is cut down in the forest of her dreams,

is she?

The sound of one heart shattering.

Mine, I guess.

All I want is to subsume her into my healing.

Absorb her darkness.

Lick her tears with a forked tongue, perhaps.

Or just hand her an apple.

The descent into hell begins.

Please fasten your seat belts

Over decrepit bones.

Direct your sockets

Heavenwards,

Not into your phones.

Fear not the demons,

The fiery cauldrons,

As you are already dead.

Dread only your fellow passengers

On the road ahead.

There is no return ticket

On this hellish ride.

Only the smoldering memories

Of your haunted pride.

<u>Return</u>

Ghosting

Like a ghost
I pass away, imprinted
In your lives
The minds and retinas of lovers
Strewn across my path
Ephemeral.

In kingdoms
Where I once ruled
Invisible
A memory of slaughtered dreams
And thwarted sunshines.

I wish to hold a hand across the Time
That sacks me.
Perchance
The apparition of a smile.
Skin flouting skin.
The bony chill of lovemaking
In search of love.

I shall be no more, I know.
No one will carry me henceforth,
Merely aspired, I am
A dissipated recollection of failed existence.

Return

About the Author

Sam Vaknin (http://samvak.tripod.com) is the author of Malignant Self-Love: Narcissism Revisited and After the Rain - How the West Lost the East, as well as many other books and ebooks about topics in psychology, relationships, philosophy, economics, and international affairs.

He was the Editor-in-Chief of Global Politician and served as a columnist for Central Europe Review, PopMatters, eBookWeb , and Bellaonline, and as a United Press International (UPI) Senior Business Correspondent. He was the editor of mental health and Central East Europe categories in The Open Directory and Suite101.

Visit Sam's Web site at http://www.narcissistic-abuse.com

Work on Narcissism

Sam Vaknin is the author of Malignant Self Love: Narcissism Revisited, the pioneering work about narcissistic abuse, now in its 10th, DSM-V compatible revision

Sam Vaknin's work is quoted in well over 1000 scholarly publications and in over 3000 books (full list here). His Narcissists, Psychopaths, and Abuse YouTube channel and other channels garnered more than 35 million views and 155,000 subscribers.

His Web site "Malignant Self Love - Narcissism Revisited" was, for many years, an Open Directory Cool Site and is a Psych-UK recommended Site.

Sam Vaknin is a professor of psychology, but he is ***not a mental health practitioner,*** though he is certified in psychological counseling techniques by Brainbench.

Sam Vaknin served as the editor of Mental Health Disorders categories in the Open Directory Project and on Mentalhelp.net. He maintains his own Websites about Narcissistic Personality Disorder (NPD) and about relationships with abusive narcissists and psychopaths here and in HealthyPlace.

You can find his work on many other Web sites: Mental Health Matters, Mental Health Sanctuary, Mental Health Today, Kathi's Mental Health Review and others.

Sam Vaknin wrote a column for Bellaonline on Narcissism and Abusive Relationships and was a frequent contributor to Websites such as Self-growth.com and Bizymoms (as an expert on personality disorders).

Sam Vaknin served as the author of the Personality Disorders topic, Narcissistic Personality Disorder topic, the Verbal and Emotional Abuse topic, and the Spousal Abuse and Domestic Violence topic, all four on Suite101. He is the moderator of the Narcissistic Abuse Study List, the Toxic Relationships Study List, and other mailing lists with a total of c. 20,000 members. He also publishes a bi-weekly Abusive Relationships Newsletter.

THE AUTHOR

Shmuel (Sam) Vaknin

Curriculum Vitae

Born in 1961 in Qiryat-Yam, Israel

Served in the Israeli Defence Force (1979-1982) in training and education units

Full proficiency in Hebrew and in English

Education

1970 to 1978

Completed nine semesters in the Technion – Israel Institute of Technology, Haifa

1982 to 1983

Ph.D. in Physics and Philosophy (dissertation: "Time Asymmetry Revisited") – California Miramar University (formerly: Pacific Western University), California, USA

1982 to 1985

Graduate of numerous courses in Finance Theory and International Trading in the UK and USA

Certified E-Commerce Concepts Analyst by Brainbench

Certified Financial Analyst by Brainbench

Certified in Psychological Counselling Techniques by Brainbench

Business Experience

1979 to 1983

Commentator in Yedioth Aharonot, Ma'ariv, and Bamakhane. Published sci-fi short fiction in Fantasy 2000.

Founder and co-owner of a chain of computerized information kiosks in Tel-Aviv, Israel.

1982 to 1985

Senior positions with the Nessim D. Gaon Group of Companies in Geneva, Paris and New-York (NOGA and APROFIM SA):

– Chief Analyst of Edible Commodities in the Group's Headquarters

– Manager of the Research and Analysis Division

– Manager of the Data Processing Division

– Project Manager of the Nigerian Computerized Census

– Vice President in charge of RND and Advanced Technologies

– Vice President in charge of Sovereign Debt Financing

1985 to 1986

Represented Canadian Venture Capital Funds in Israel

1986 to 1987

General Manager of IPE Ltd. in London. The firm financed international multi-lateral countertrade and leasing transactions.

1988 to 1990

Co-founder and Director of "Mikbats-Tesuah", a portfolio management firm based in Tel-Aviv.

Activities included large-scale portfolio management, underwriting, forex trading and general financial advisory services.

1990 to Present

Freelance consultant to many of Israel's Blue-Chip firms, mainly on issues related to the capital markets in Israel, Canada, the UK and the USA.

Consultant to foreign RND ventures and to Governments on macro-economic matters.

Freelance journalist in various media in the United States.

1990 to 1995

President of the Israel chapter of the Professors World Peace Academy (PWPA) and (briefly) Israel representative of the "Washington Times".

1993 to 1994

Co-owner and Director of many business enterprises:

– The Omega and Energy Air-conditioning Concern

– AVP Financial Consultants

– Handiman Legal Services – Total annual turnover of the group: 10 million USD.

Co-owner, Director and Finance Manager of COSTI Ltd. – Israel's largest computerized information vendor and developer. Raised funds through a series of private placements locally in the USA, Canada and London.

1993 to 1996

Publisher and Editor of a Capital Markets Newsletter distributed by subscription only to dozens of subscribers countrywide.

Tried and incarcerated for 11 months for his role in an attempted takeover of Israel's Agriculture Bank involving securities fraud.

Managed the Internet and International News Department of an Israeli mass media group, "Ha-Tikshoret and Namer".

Assistant in the Law Faculty in Tel-Aviv University (to Prof. S.G. Shoham)

1996 to 1999

Financial consultant to leading businesses in Macedonia, Russia and the Czech Republic.

Economic commentator in "Nova Makedonija", "Dnevnik", "Makedonija Denes", "Izvestia", "Argumenti i Fakti", "The Middle East Times", "The New Presence", "Central Europe Review", and other periodicals, and in the economic programs on various channels of Macedonian Television.

Chief Lecturer in courses in Macedonia organized by the Agency of Privatization, by the Stock Exchange, and by the Ministry of Trade.

1999 to 2002
Economic Advisor to the Government of the Republic of Macedonia and to the Ministry of Finance.

2001 to 2003
Senior Business Correspondent for United Press International (UPI)

2005 to Present
Associate Editor and columnist, Global Politician

Founding Analyst, The Analyst Network

Contributing Writer, The American Chronicle Media Group

Expert, Self-growth and Bizymoms and contributor to Mental Health Matters

2007 to 2008
Columnist and analyst in "Nova Makedonija", "Fokus", and "Kapital" (Macedonian papers and newsweeklies)

2008 to 2011
Member of the Steering Committee for the Advancement of Healthcare in the Republic of Macedonia

Advisor to the Minister of Health of Macedonia

Seminars and lectures on economic issues in various forums in Macedonia

Contributor to CommentVision

2011 to Present
Editor in Chief of Global Politician and Investment Politics

Columnist in Dnevnik and Publika, Fokus, and Nova Makedonija (Macedonia)

Columnist in InfoPlus and Libertas

Member CFACT Board of Advisors

Contributor to Recovering the Self

Columnist in New York Daily Sun

Teaches at CIAPS (Center for International and Advanced Professional Studies)

2017 to 2022
Visiting Professor of Psychology in Southern Federal University, Rostov-on-Don, Russia

Web and Journalistic Activities

Author of extensive Web sites in:

– Psychology ("Malignant Self-love: Narcissism Revisited") – an Open Directory Cool Site for 8
  years

– Philosophy ("Philosophical Musings")

– Economics and Geopolitics ("World in Conflict and Transition")

Owner of the Narcissistic Abuse Study List, the Toxic Relationships List, and the Abusive
Relationships Newsletter (more than 8000 members)

Owner of the Economies in Conflict and Transition Study List and the Links and Factoid Study List

Editor of mental health disorders and Central and Eastern Europe categories in various Web
directories (Open Directory, Search Europe, Mentalhelp.net)

Editor of the Personality Disorders, Narcissistic Personality Disorder, the Verbal and Emotional
Abuse, and the Spousal (Domestic) Abuse and Violence topics on Suite 101 and contributing author
on Bellaonline.

Columnist and commentator in "The New Presence", United Press International (UPI),
InternetContent, eBookWeb, PopMatters, Global Politician, The Analyst Network, Conservative
Voice, The American Chronicle Media Group, eBookNet.org, and "Central Europe Review".

Publications and Awards

"Managing Investment Portfolios in States of Uncertainty", Limon Publishers, Tel-Aviv, 1988

"The Gambling Industry", Limon Publishers, Tel-Aviv, 1990

"Requesting My Loved One: Short Stories", Miskal-Yedioth Aharonot, Tel-Aviv, 1997

"The Suffering of Being Kafka" (electronic book of Hebrew and English Short Fiction), Prague,
1998-2004

"The Macedonian Economy at a Crossroads – On the Way to a Healthier Economy" (dialogues with
Nikola Gruevski), Skopje, 1998

"The Exporter's Pocketbook" Ministry of Trade, Republic of Macedonia, Skopje, 1999

"Malignant Self-love: Narcissism Revisited", Narcissus Publications, Prague and Skopje, 1999-2015

The Narcissism, Psychopathy, and Abuse in Relationships Series (electronic books regarding
relationships with abusive narcissists and psychopaths), Prague, 1999-2015

"After the Rain – How the West Lost the East", Narcissus Publications in association with Central
Europe Review/CEENMI, Prague and Skopje, 2000

Personality Disorders Revisited (electronic book about personality disorders), Prague, 2007

More than 30 e-books about psychology, international affairs, business and economics, philosophy, short fiction, and reference

Winner of numerous awards, among them Israel's Council of Culture and Art Prize for Maiden Prose (1997), The Rotary Club Award for Social Studies (1976), and the Bilateral Relations Studies Award of the American Embassy in Israel (1978).

Hundreds of professional articles in all fields of finance and economics, and numerous articles dealing with geopolitical and political economic issues, published in both print and Web periodicals in many countries.

Many appearances in the electronic and print media on subjects in psychology, philosophy, and the sciences, and concerning economic matters.

Citations via Google Scholar page:

http://scholar.google.com/citations?user=Yj7C8wOP-10J

Write to Me:
samvaknin@gmail.com

narcissisticabuse-owner@yahoogroups.com

My Web Sites:
Economy/Politics:
http://ceeandbalkan.tripod.com/

Psychology:
http://www.narcissistic-abuse.com/

Philosophy:
http://philosophos.tripod.com/

Poetry:
http://samvak.tripod.com/contents.html

Fiction:
http://samvak.tripod.com/sipurim.html

Follow my work on NARCISSISTS and PSYCHOPATHS

As well as commentaries on international affairs and economics

My work in Psychology: Media Kit and Press Room

http://www.narcissistic-abuse.com/mediakit.html

Biography and Resume

http://www.narcissistic-abuse.com/cv.html

Be my friend on **Facebook**:

http://www.facebook.com/samvaknin

https://www.facebook.com/narcissismwithvaknin/ **(personal page)**

Subscribe to my **YouTube** channel (620+ videos about narcissists and psychopaths and abuse in relationships):

http://www.youtube.com/samvaknin

https://www.youtube.com/user/samvaknin/community (Community)

Follow me on **Instagram**:

https://www.instagram.com/narcissismwithvaknin/ (active)

https://www.instagram.com/vakninsamnarcissist/ (archive)

Read my **Blog**:

http://narcissistpsychopathabuse.blogspot.mk

http://narcissistpsychopathabuse.blogspot.com

Subscribe to my **other YouTube channel** (200+ videos about international affairs, economics, and philosophy):

http://www.youtube.com/vakninmusings

You may also join **Malignant Self-love: Narcissism Revisited on Facebook**:

http://www.facebook.com/pages/Malignant-Self-Love-Narcissism-Revisited/50634038043 or https://www.facebook.com/NarcissusPublications

http://www.facebook.com/narcissistpsychopathabuse

Follow me on **Linkedin, Twitter, MySpace, Pinterest, Tumblr, Minds, and Ello**:

http://www.linkedin.com/in/samvaknin

http://www.twitter.com/samvaknin

http://www.myspace.com/samvaknin

http://pinterest.com/samvaknin/the-psychopathic-narcissist-and-his-world/

http://narcissistpsychopath-abuse.tumblr.com/

https://www.minds.com/samvaknin

https://ello.co/malignantselflove

https://ello.co/samvaknin

Subscribe to my **Scribd** page: dozens of books for download at no cost to you!

http://www.scribd.com/samvaknin

Zadanliran is following my work as well:

http://www.scribd.com/zadanliran

Additional Resources

Testimonials and Additional Resources

You can read hundreds of Readers' Reviews at the Barnes and Noble, and Amazon Web pages dedicated to "Malignant Self-love" - HERE:

https://www.amazon.com/dp/1983208175 (Amazon US)

https://www.amazon.co.uk/dp/1983208175 (Amazon UK)

Participate in discussions about Abusive Relationships:

http://www.runboard.com/bnarcissisticabuserecovery

http://thepsychopath.freeforums.org/

Abusive Relationships Newsletters

http://groups.google.com/group/narcissisticabuse/

https://groups.google.com/g/narcissistic-personality-disorder

To purchase from Amazon use this link:

http://www.amazon.com/Malignant-Self-Love-Narcissism-Sam-Vaknin/dp/8023833847

II. ELECTRONIC BOOKS (e-Books)

From KINDLE (AMAZON)

Kindle Books about Narcissists, Psychopaths, and Abusive Relationships – use these links:

http://www.amazon.com/s/ref=ntt_athr_dp_sr_1?_encoding=UTF8&field-author=Sam%20Vaknin&search-alias=digital-text&sort=relevancerank (Amazon USA)

http://www.amazon.co.uk/s/ref=ntt_athr_dp_sr_1?_encoding=UTF8&field-author=Sam%20Vaknin&search-alias=digital-text&sort=relevancerank (Amazon UK)

BUY SIXTEEN e-books about toxic relationships with narcissists and psychopaths - and get the PDF versions of ALL 16 books plus a huge bonus pack FREE!

Use either of these links and send the proof of purchase via email to samvaknin@gmail.com to receive the PDFs and Bonus Pack:

https://www.amazon.com/dp/B07FK6316T (Amazon USA)

https://www.amazon.co.uk/dp/B07FK6316T (Amazon UK)

III. Cold Therapy Seminar on DVDs

http://www.narcissistic-abuse.com/ctcounsel.html

IV. Counselling with Sam Vaknin or Lidija Rangelovska (or both)

http://www.narcissistic-abuse.com/ctcounsel.html

Free excerpts from the EIGHTH, Revised Impression of "Malignant Self-love: Narcissism Revisited" are available as well as a **NEW EDITION of the Narcissism Book of Quotes**.

Use this link to download the files:

http://www.narcissistic-abuse.com/freebooks.html

Download Free Electronic Books on this link:

http://www.narcissistic-abuse.com/freebooks.html

Return

9 798421 460404